CW00793792

Murder and the Pantomime Cat

Lesley Cookman

Published by Accent Press Ltd 2018
Octavo House
West Bute Street
Cardiff
CF10 5LJ

www.accentpress.co.uk

ISBN: 9781786157478

eISBN: 9781786156891

'Puss is very good,' Fran Wolfe whispered to Libby Sarjeant. 'Is he a friend of Andrew's?'

'Don't know,' whispered back Libby. 'Shh – I want to hear this bit.'

The auditorium of The Alexandria was almost empty, except for Libby, Fran, the pantomime director, the lighting director talking incessantly on his headset to his operatives, the wardrobe mistress, who kept darting in and out, and a couple of cast members who weren't on yet.

'And make way for Princess Pam!' a small member of the chorus was declaiming in a squeaky voice.

Princess Pam, in a vaguely eighteenth-century costume, entered somewhat nervously, obviously very aware of Puss, at the side of the stage, mimicking both the announcement and her entrance. Libby felt uncomfortable. This didn't look as though it was the director's idea, more as if Puss was building his part. She glanced at Fran and saw that she felt the same.

1

The King and Queen followed her onto the stage.

'Clemency's nervous, too,' whispered Fran.

'Bloody King isn't!' Libby growled back. 'Smarmy git.'

The director sent them a fulminating glare, and they shrank down in their seats.

This was the dress rehearsal for The Alexandria's first pantomime, and due to Libby and Fran's association with the theatre, the management company had called on them for help. They, in turn, had called on two of their professional colleagues in the world of theatre, Sir Andrew McColl and Dame Amanda Knight, to help with recruitment. Nethergate, the seaside town which was home to both Fran and The Alexandria, a former concert hall, wasn't a big player in the resort world, and hadn't attracted any of the larger pantomime production companies, so the management company was bravely going it alone. The cast Andrew and Amanda – or Abby, as Libby had known her in childhood – had helped assemble contained a few names well known to the public, although it remained to be seen if they would still be as popular now as in their heydays.

The most current personality in the cast - apart from the perennially popular Tom, the Miller's Son - was the nervous Princess Pam, a reality TV star. Tom presented a weekday programme on children's television, and Princess Pam visibly relaxed as he moved towards her, blocking her view of Puss.

The King stepped in front of the Queen and the Chamberlain and spread his arms. 'Hello, Royal subjects!' he declaimed, a characteristic giggle in his well-trained voice.

'Ugh!' said Libby, scowling at the stage. Fran dug her in the ribs.

The scene wore on, with both the King and Puss doing their best to upstage everyone else, until at last Puss led the cast in a predictable chorus number about boots and walking and the director, sounding depressed, called a halt.

Libby and Fran left the auditorium and went out on to the little gallery that ran round the back of the theatre, overlooking Nethergate beach.

'He's going to have to put a stop to all that,' said Libby, hunching her shoulders inside her new mock-fur trimmed cape. 'It's just a collection of egos and nerves up there at the moment.'

Fran leant her elbows on the railings and gazed out to sea. 'I don't know why he hasn't done it already.'

'Scared of them walking,' said Libby. 'Puss is notorious for bad behaviour, isn't he?'

'So Dame Amanda said.'

'Oh, do stop calling her that.' Libby frowned. 'She's Abby. I always called her Abby, and she asked you to, as well.'

'It seems disrespectful, somehow.' Fran turned her back on the sea. 'And why is he picking on that poor little girl?'

Libby shrugged. 'Anyone with a weakness is fair game, I suppose. And she's not a Proper

4

Actor, is she?'

'Such a shame,' said Fran. 'She needs the support of the cast. If he's so set against having reality stars in the show, the least he could do is simply ignore her. He's just making her even more nervous.'

'Which is the whole point,' said Libby. 'He's hoping she loses her nerve completely and makes a fool of herself.'

'That will upset everybody,' said Fran.

'Except the avuncular King.' Libby pondered. 'That would give him the opportunity to be all kind and protective and "look what a lovely guy I am" in front of the audience.'

Fran nodded. 'He's not giving Clemency much of a chance, is he?'

Clemency, playing the Queen, was coming back to the stage after a few years' 'finding herself'. As Dame Amanda's daughter, she had always felt overshadowed by her mother, but had accepted the part despite Dame Amanda having been instrumental in putting it her way.

'No – he's playing up to the image he's been cultivating for the last ten or fifteen years. Lovely, cuddly Cooper – the ladies all love him.' Libby struck an attitude. 'And hasn't he got a lovely voice?' She dropped the falsetto and growled, 'Have you heard his radio show? It's nauseating!'

'Don't hold back, will you?' Fran was amused. 'At least young what's-his-name – Tom – seems a nice bloke.'

'Apparently he is. Both Andrew and Abby know him. RADA-trained apparently, and quite content to play Shakespeare secondaries until someone spotted him as TV material. The kids love him.'

Fran cocked an eyebrow. 'Too good to be true?'

'I don't think so.' Libby sighed. 'Shall we go in and see if they're starting again?'

'I think I'd rather leave it and come and see it when it's running. You go in if you want to.'

'No, I think I agree with you.' Libby settled

the cape round her neck. 'I'll give Andrew a ring and tell him. He can tell Abby.'

'When are we supposed to be going?' asked Fran as they walked up the slope to Victoria Place.

'Officially, with Abby and Andrew on Saturday. We can go in whenever we like after that. If they haven't sold out.'

'Will they? Sell out, I mean.'

Libby shrugged. 'It's selling well so far. After all, they've got young Holly Westcott, Cooper Fallon, and whosit playing Tom.'

'Mark Jones,' said Fran. 'And old Richard Brandon playing the Ogre. He was in that soap for years, wasn't he? He's popular.'

'Well, there you are. And they've got Sheila Bernard as the fairy, Gawd 'elp 'em. Diva of Divas.'

'She's killing it, isn't she?' said Fran. 'It's supposed to be a comedy part.'

'And she's making it into high drama,' said Libby. 'Ah, well. Nowt to do with us, is it, chuck? Let's just hope they can sort out their differences and stagger on until after Christmas.'

Libby scoured the internet after the first night of *Puss in Boots*, but found nothing. Eventually, tracking down the social media accounts of some of the cast members, she was able to get a sense of the atmosphere, which didn't seem as positive as she would have hoped.

Young Holly had said nothing, Cooper Fallon had been self-congratulatory, Clemency was brightly humorous, Sheila Bernard had been dramatic, and the rest had sensibly kept quiet. Libby phoned Fran.

'Yes, I looked, too. Doesn't look too good, does it?'

'Perhaps it'll settle in,' said Libby, without much hope. 'Only two weeks' rehearsal, after all…'

'They're professionals,' said Fran. 'That's all they ever get for panto.'

'I know.' Libby heaved a sigh. 'And I've got

just over that left for mine.'

Libby's own production of *Sleeping Beauty* at the Oast Theatre in Steeple Martin was trundling along in a much happier atmosphere.

'But everyone knows what they're doing, and how it's going to run,' said Fran. 'After all – how many years have you been doing it? And so have most of the cast.'

'Mmm. Anyway – did you find any mention anywhere of the cast?'

'No. But do they actually do reviews anywhere? The *Stage*?'

Libby thought for a moment. 'Well, they do, but not straight away, unless it's top-flight West End. There must be online sites, though. I'm just not well up on them.'

'Ask Jane?' suggested Fran. Jane Baker was the Deputy Editor of the now mostly online *Nethergate Mercury*, and a longstanding friend.

'Oh, I don't like to bother her,' said Libby.

'Send her a text. She can answer or not.'

'OK, I'll do that. It's not really important, is

it?' said Libby, while feeling that somehow, it probably was.

But even before Libby had laboriously sent Jane a text, not being as handy with her thumbs as some, her mobile rang.

'Libby? It's Clemency – Clemency Knight.'

'Clemency!' Libby's eyebrows rose. 'How lovely to hear from you. What can I do for you? I'm coming to see you on Saturday.'

'Yes, I know, with Mum and Andrew,' said Clemency, sounding depressed.

Libby was stumped. From Clemency's tone, the right question would not be 'How's it going?'

'Fran and I saw some of the dress,' she said eventually.

'Yes.' The word came out on a sigh. 'Actually, Libby, it was the show I wanted to talk to you about.'

'Oh?' said Libby warily.

'Well, you had something do with the show, didn't you? Casting and so on?'

'A bit. We're on the management committee, Fran and me. An honorary position, really.' This wasn't the time to go into the reasons they were there, she felt.

'You see, I don't know who else to talk to. I don't want to tell Mum, so…'

'You thought you'd tell us? Me and Fran?'

'Yes.' Clemency sounded grateful.

Libby stifled a sigh. This didn't bode well. 'OK – where are you lodging? Shall we come there?'

'No, no,' said Clemency hastily. 'I'm staying with Mum and Coolidge. I'll meet you in Nethergate somewhere, shall I? As long as it's not near where the others are staying.'

'And where's that?'

'Cooper Fallon and Holly Westcott are at Anderson Place – do you know it? – and Brandon, Sheila, and Tom are at The Swan.'

'What about Puss?'

'Ackroyd? He's got digs.' Libby heard a snort. 'He likes to keep up the myth of the old time performer. Except that it's a luxury service flat.'

'Right.' The more Libby got to know about Puss the less she liked him. 'Well, probably best to meet at Fran's house, if she's agreeable. I'll ask and ring you back, shall I?'

'Yes…' Clemency hesitated. 'When? I mean when could we meet?'

'When have you got matinees?'

'Tomorrow. I could come in the morning.'

'OK. I'll ring you back as soon as I can.'

Fran was quite happy for Clemency to come for coffee the following morning, if slightly puzzled. 'You'll be here before she arrives, though, won't you? About quarter to eleven?'

'Yes – and I don't know what it is she wants to talk about, either. She doesn't like Puss, though. Ackroyd something his name is.'

'Ah, yes. Ackroyd Lee, I remember now. I did something with him years ago. I don't suppose he'd remember me.'

'Was he doing skin parts then?'

'No – he was lowly chorus! A good dancer, though. I was second juve.'

'Ooh, tell me more.'

'No fear. Makes me feel very, very old. Let me know if she's coming.'

Clemency was indeed coming and sounded very pleased to be doing so.

'I wonder what's up?' Libby asked Sidney the cat, as she wandered into the conservatory to stare at the unfinished landscape on her easel. 'Why us?'

Sidney came to stare at the landscape too, just in case he got an extra treat for appreciation.

Then Libby remembered she had been going to send Jane Baker a text, and decided to phone her instead. Sidney left in a huff.

'Sorry if I'm disturbing you,' she said.

'You aren't. I'm at home,' said Jane. 'You know I do a lot of work at home now. What can I do for you?'

'I don't always want a favour,' said Libby, a little put out.

'What, then?' said Jane, sounding amused. 'Asking after my health?'

'I just wondered if you or someone else was going to see *Puss in Boots* at The Alexandria.'

'We've got comps, why?'

'When for?'

'Look, Lib, what *is* this? Why are you interested?'

'I just wondered. Fran and I are going with Sir Andrew and Dame Amanda on Saturday.'

'Oh, of course – you helped with casting, didn't you?'

'Not really, Andrew and Abby did, but we got them involved.'

'And you're still on the steering committee, too, aren't you? Or whatever it's called.'

'Management committee, I think, but we don't have to do much.'

'So why do you want to know if the *Mercury* is turning up? Persuading us to give a good review?'

'I was hoping you'd already have heard...'

Libby tailed off. Heard what? She scowled at the floor. 'If you'd heard what anybody thought?'

'Anybody?' Libby heard the laugh in Jane's voice. 'No, I haven't. I'll ask in the office, if you like. Can't be too bad, can it? They've got some names in there.'

'Yes,' said Libby dubiously. 'Oh, well, I'll let you know what we think after Saturday.'

'And I'll let you know what our official line is after someone's seen it from here.'

'OK. Love to Immi and Terry.' Libby rang off. 'Come on, Sid. Time for tea.' Tail high, Sidney took up his station by the treats shelf.

The following morning, Libby parked almost opposite Coastguard Cottage in Harbour Street, Nethergate and waved at Balzac, Fran's black and white cat, who was sitting in the bay window.

'What do you suppose she wants?' asked Libby, following Fran into the kitchen, where a very new coffee machine was standing by the sink.

'It's challenging me,' said Fran, eyeing it with disfavour.

'Why did you buy it, then?'

'I didn't. Sophie bought it for us as an anniversary present. Do you want to have a go?'

'No, thank you, you know I don't much like coffee. Will you try and make a cup for Clemency?'

'Probably not.' Fran threw a tea towel over the offending item. 'Instant, it'll be. Unless she wants tea. OK – so back to your question. What does she want?'

'To talk to someone who isn't her mother,' said Libby. 'She probably feels ungrateful because she's not enjoying it.'

'Did you get the sense that it was anyone in particular annoying her?'

'She didn't say, but she obviously doesn't like Ackroyd. Mind you, we saw what his behaviour was like at the dress, didn't we?' Libby perched on the edge of the table.

'You don't think she wants us to actually *do*

something, do you?' Fran looked nervous.

'Do what? There isn't anything to look into, surely?'

'Well, she's coming to see us about *some*thing, isn't she?'

There was a sharp rap on the door and they both jumped.

'That'll be her now,' said Libby. 'Shall I let her in?'

Clemency stood outside looking even more nervous than Fran. She'd lost weight since they'd last met her at Mallowan Manor four years ago, and without her queenly costume she looked pale and unremarkable.

'Come in,' said Libby, trying not to smile too brightly.

'Coffee?' offered Fran, with a shifty glance towards the lurking machine.

'I'd prefer tea, if you don't mind,' said Clemency hesitantly.

'Lovely – so would I,' said Libby. Fran made a face.

'Now, Clemency.' Libby indicated the squashy sofa in front of the fireplace. 'What did you want to talk to us about?'

'It's rather difficult.' Clemency looked down at her hands. 'It's probably just that I've been out of the business for a few years.'

'What is?'

'What's what?' Now Clemency looked bewildered.

'*What's* because you've been out of the business?'

'The atmosphere. Well -' she came to a halt as Fran came in with three mugs.

'Well?' prompted Libby.

'Ackroyd, mostly.'

Libby and Fran exchanged glances.

'Oh, I know Ackroyd Lee,' said Fran, passing over a mug.

'Lee?' Clemency now looked startled. 'Oh, no, his name's Lane. Ackroyd Lane.'

'Well, it wasn't,' said Fran. 'He was chorus last time I saw him, and his name was Ackroyd

Lee. I always thought it was a peculiar name – Ackroyd.'

Libby made a mental note to look into this anomaly.

'So what's the problem?' she asked. 'We saw some of his antics at the dress. Very unprofessional.'

'He's terrifying little Holly,' said Clemency, ignoring the fact that she was a good three inches shorter than the principal girl.

'We noticed,' said Libby. 'Why hasn't the director put a stop to it?'

'He tried.' Clemency shook her head. 'But Ackroyd just smiles – you, know, like he does – and ignores him. The trouble is, the kids love him.'

'It's not just him, though, is it?' asked Fran shrewdly.

Clemency sighed. 'No. I don't know whether it's because I never used to do panto before, but I've never experienced this sort of thing.'

'Always more of a collaborative ensemble

thing, eh?' suggested Libby.

'Exactly.' Clemency turned to her thankfully. 'No stars, if you know what I mean. But in this one there seem to be too many. Did you hear about the row over billing?'

'No.'

'Cooper Fallon and Holly were more or less sharing top billing, and as they're both sort of current, that seemed fair. Old Brandon didn't mind, neither did Mark, and quite honestly, I would have said he was more popular than all of them put together.' She sighed again. 'But Ackroyd kicked up a terrible fuss, and Sheila did, too. She said if Ackroyd was put up, so should she be.'

'Why did Ackroyd think he should have top billing?' asked Fran. 'He does skin parts. It's not *Hamlet*.'

'He was in a long-running kids show on TV.'

'Well, Mark Jones still is. Was it very popular?' asked Libby.

'Haven't you heard of *Raggedy Cat*?' asked

Clemency in astonishment. 'Ackroyd *is* Raggedy Cat.'

'Oh!' Libby and Fran were enlightened. Even they hadn't managed to miss the phenomenon that had spread black and white cat images over everything from pyjamas to lunch boxes.

'But surely,' said Libby, 'it's no longer on TV. He rather lost popularity, didn't he?'

'I don't know about that,' said Clemency, 'but he's still regarded as a top notch skin player.'

'OK. What about Cooper Fallon?' asked Fran. 'Did he kick up a fuss?'

'When he thought Ackroyd might get top billing, yes. He's a current radio personality...' she trailed off.

'Embarrassing?' suggested Libby.

'It was, rather,' said Clemency with a shamefaced grin.

'I don't know why Sheila got uppity, though.' Fran frowned. 'She's only really a stage star, isn't she?'

'And not the young star she used to be,' agreed Libby.

'Mum used to know her,' said Clemency. 'They did Shakespeare together years ago. Mum was Gertrude and she was Ophelia, and they did several Ayckbourns in the West End.'

'Oh, I thought she'd concentrated on musicals,' said Libby. 'So much for being in the business myself.'

'Well, anyway,' Clemency went on, 'the atmosphere's been dreadful. Ackroyd's playing every nasty trick he can think of, Sheila's ignoring everyone and cutting people's lines, and Cooper's putting in so many bits of business he's ruining every scene. Especially,' she concluded gloomily, 'mine.'

'Sounds awful,' said Libby, glancing at Fran. 'But what do you want us to do about it?'

Silence fell. Clemency gazed first at the floor, then at Fran and, finally, at Libby.

'I don't know.' She fidgeted with her mug. 'But you helped Mum over that business at

Mallowan Manor…'

'Yes, but there was something concrete going on there, wasn't there?' said Libby. 'We can't investigate atmosphere.'

'And we can't interfere with the production, either,' said Fran. 'Sir Andrew or your mother might be able to have a word with the director, but only after they've seen for themselves.'

'I didn't want to worry Mum.'

'Who appointed the director?' asked Libby.

'I don't know. Mum and Coolidge seem to know all about him.'

'Could we ask Coolidge, do you think?' Libby looked across at Fran. 'I bet he knows as much as the others.'

'More, usually,' said Clemency, with a faint smile.

'Do you mind if we do? Ask him, I mean,' said Fran.

'No, I suppose not.' Clemency made a face. 'He's always been very good to all of us, and he never seems to mind that he gave up his own career for Mum's.'

Coolidge had first been presented to Libby and Fran as Dame Amanda's butler, in the impeccable mould of PG Wodehouse's Jeeves. It transpired that this was an act put on to impress the susceptible and they in fact had been married, by that time, for several years.

'I don't see how we can ask him without Dame Amanda knowing,' said Fran.

'No.' Libby and Fran both turned inquiring gazes on Clemency, who looked resigned.

'Oh, well, do your best. Only I don't think I can carry on until after Christmas like this, and Mum will think…'

'Think what? She's your mother!' said Libby.

'But I don't want to go running to Mummy! And that's what the rest of the cast will think.'

'No reason for them to know,' said Libby bracingly. 'Now, come on. Time you were getting off to the theatre, even if you don't want to.'

When Clemency had gone, Fran and Libby

sat silent for a while. Eventually Fran got up to clear away the mugs.

'Go on, then,' she said. 'Ring Coolidge.'

Libby sighed, dug out her mobile and scrolled through to find the number.

'I hope we're doing the right thing,' she said, as she waited to connect.

'Hello, Libby?' Coolidge's quiet tones were instantly soothing. 'Did you want Abby?'

'No, Coolidge, actually it's you I wanted. And it's rather difficult.'

'Ah.' There was a smile in Coolidge's voice. 'Clemency, then?'

'How did you know?' gasped Libby.

'It's been fairly obvious that the panto isn't going well. But she won't tell her mother what's wrong, and by extension, me. So what's the problem?'

As succinctly as she could, Libby explained, including hers and Fran's impressions from the dress rehearsal.

'What does she want you to do?' asked

Coolidge, when she'd finished.

'Put a stop to it, I suppose,' said Libby. 'But goodness knows how. I mean, when I was still in the business full time, this sort of thing cropped up, but never in such a wholesale form, and it usually got sorted out. I don't know what we're supposed to do. The director should do something, really, shouldn't he? Do you know him?'

'Yes.' Coolidge sighed. 'He's another of Abby's lame ducks. She worked with him several years ago, and he had a run of bad luck. He isn't used to panto – that's one of the problems.'

'Blimey! And it's not as if he's got an experienced team around him, is it? The choreography looked all right, and the music sounded OK, but they aren't used to working together, are they?'

'Actually the MD and choreographer are. They came as a package, so hopefully they've been a bit of help. But I'll see what I can do. I don't suppose I can do it without Abby knowing, though.'

'No, that's what I told Clemency, but she doesn't want to be seen to go running to Mummy.'

'Leave it with me. When is it we're all going? Tomorrow, isn't it? I'll try and have a word or two before then.'

Libby reported this conversation to Fran, who shook her head. 'I've got a bad feeling about this.'

'Oh, come on! That's what they say in the movies!'

'No, but I have.' Fran frowned at her friend. 'There's a nasty undercurrent.'

Libby shifted uneasily in her chair. 'Well, yes…'

'I just hope no one gets damaged.'

'Damaged? What do you mean?'

'It could mean anything.' Fran shook her head again. 'But someone's going to be hurt.'

'Clemency and Holly already are,' said

Libby.

On Saturday evening, Guy and Ben had politely declined to accompany Libby and Fran to the pantomime, but had elected to spend the evening in Nethergate's plentiful pubs. Libby and Ben were to stay overnight.

They were duly met in the foyer of The Alexandria by the current manager, who bore them away to an upper room where Dame Amanda, Coolidge, and Sir Andrew were all waiting, glasses of champagne in hand. The director was also there, looking distinctly ill at ease.

'Any luck?' Libby managed to whisper to Coolidge.

He shrugged. 'Tell you later. Difficult.'

After a few formal words of thanks, the small party were ushered away to prime seats in the stalls and the house lights were dimmed.

'Here we go,' Libby whispered, and Fran dug her in the ribs.

At first, everything seemed to be going well. Tom the Miller's Son had the children in the audience on his side from the word go, the mischievous Puss had everyone alternately cheering and booing, and Princess Pam was endearingly shy. The King, admittedly, was a little overbearing towards his charmingly daffy Queen, and the Fairy was positively Wagnerian, but all in all, Libby was pleasantly surprised.

However, things began to change after the first 'front of tabs' scene. This was a scene played in front of the curtain to facilitate a change of scene behind, and in this case by the two funny men, or Broker's Men as they were in *Cinderella*. They had worked together for years and knew just how to wind the audience up. But the cheerful atmosphere crashed apart on the opening of the riverbank scene, where Puss was supposed to persuade Tom to remove his clothes and jump in the river. Only Puss wasn't playing.

The little party in the stalls moved uneasily in their seats as Puss pursued his own course through the scene with poor Tom struggling to catch up and get back on track, a feat only accomplished by the funny men making an unscheduled appearance and kidnapping the cat. The rest of the audience didn't appear to notice anything wrong, and Tom managed to play the rest of the scene on his own, until the entrance of the Royal Party, at which point the party in the stalls all looked at each other in desperation.

Here, Puss was supposed to rush out in his guise as 'the servant of the Marquis of Carrabas', and solicit the King's help. The funny men, proving themselves to be true professionals, once again saved the day by bringing on a bound and gagged Puss and telling the King they had caught him *pretending* to be the servant of the Marquis of Carrabas. That Puss was furious could be plainly seen, but the delighted audience just cheered the funny men on, Tom was 'rescued' from the river and provided with new clothes, and the scene ended traditionally, with a rousing chorus number.

After another front cloth scene and the palace scene where the Ogre captures the princess, it was the interval, and Libby's party made thankfully for the bar.

'I don't know if I can stand the second half,' said Dame Amanda, accepting a glass of wine from an attentive minion. 'How could I have sent poor Clemency into that hellhole?'

'None of us were to know,' said Sir Andrew. 'I feel terrible because I recommended Ackroyd Lane.'

'Do you know him?' asked Fran.

'Not personally, simply by reputation as a good skin part player. And to tell the truth, I felt a bit sorry for him. After they cancelled his telly, he couldn't get arrested.'

'Do you know why they cancelled it?' asked Coolidge.

'There were rumours,' said Sir Andrew darkly, 'but aren't there always?'

'And Cooper Fallon,' mused Dame Amanda. 'His star has been falling a bit recently, hasn't it? He can't play the big musical leads any more, and he doesn't want to do G&S, although when we did *The Mikado* together he was a lovely Mikado.'

'I didn't realise you'd done G&S,' said Libby. 'Were you Katisha?'

'Who else?' Amanda grinned. 'This was a few years ago, and I don't think Cooper liked playing father to someone old enough to be his mother!'

'You weren't,' said Coolidge. 'He isn't that young.'

Amanda turned to Libby and Fran. 'I wasn't sure what to believe when Coolidge told me Clem had been to see you. I put it down to nerves – but now I've seen it…' She shook her head. 'Actually she's coping very well.'

'She is,' said Fran. 'She's turned herself into a long-suffering Queen, hasn't she?'

'I wonder how they've coped with Puss in the interval?' said Coolidge. 'We've got the big Lion and Mouse sequence coming up, haven't

32

we? How will he deal with that one?'

But to everyone's surprise, Puss behaved impeccably, although turning in a less than inspired performance. Dame Amanda sent a message round to Clemency saying they would see her in the bar of The Swan on the square rather than in the theatre, in order to avoid confrontation with any of the other stars or the management. As it happened, Ben and Guy were also in there, and looked rather surprised to see them. Libby went over to explain and, at Sir Andrew's request, to ask them to join them. Coolidge surprised everybody by ordering champagne, which, he explained, was to assure Clemency that her own performance was above reproach.

She arrived, surprisingly, with young Mark Jones in tow.

'I knew you wouldn't mind, mum,' she said, after a round of kisses had been exchanged. 'And Mark's been suffering as much as any of us in the last few days.'

'He didn't have a go at you tonight, though,' said Libby. 'What -'

She was cut off simultaneously by a kick from Fran, a glare from Ben and Sir Andrew rushing into speech. She subsided.

'What we want to know,' said Sir Andrew, 'is what happened in the interval. I was almost sure you'd have to go on without a Puss.'

Clemency and Mark looked at one another.

'We don't know,' said Mark. 'Pinch and Punch wouldn't let him go and carted him off to one of the dressing rooms, where our dear director apparently read the riot act. He was warned that if he stepped out of line, Pinch and Punch would make another unscheduled entrance and haul him off for the rest of the show. I don't know how Sam made him promise. He isn't the strongest director in the world.'

'Counter-blackmail?' suggested Clemency, then looked stricken, as all the guests turned to her in horror.

'Blackmail?' chorused Dame Amanda, Fran, and Libby together.

Mark sighed, and seemed to slump in his chair. 'Oh, yes. That was one of his choicest tricks. Sly little suggestions that he knew something disreputable about you.'

'And the trouble was,' said Clemency, 'there was just enough truth there to get you wondering.'

'He couldn't have had anything on you, darling,' said Dame Amanda, while Coolidge took her hand.

'Oh, I got my part through nepotism, apparently, not having enough talent to make it on my own.' Clemency screwed up her face.

'As host of a kids' TV show, you can imagine what my crime was supposed to be,' said Mark gloomily. 'However,' he said, brightening, 'I threw the same things back at him about his own show. That shut him up as far as I was concerned, but I bet he would have found another little stick to prod me with.'

'And what will happen now?' asked Fran.

'He's staying, apparently,' said Clemency. 'At least for tomorrow's shows, to see how he behaves.'

The two shows on Sundays were at 10.30 in the morning and 2.30 in the afternoon, and universally loathed by casts from the West End downwards.

'Has he got an understudy?' asked Coolidge.

'We've all got chorus understudies,' said Mark. 'They can't afford anything else, but we have to have them, or we don't get any time off. Not that we take time off, of course, unless it's illness or the traditional granny's funeral.'

'So is that the problem with everyone? A little bit of homely blackmail?' asked Libby.

'It isn't really blackmail,' said Clemency. 'He doesn't *want* anything. Just to make you aware he has a hold over you. Or thinks he has.'

'He hasn't got a hold over poor little Holly,' said Mark. 'He just delights in playing every trick in the book and unnerving her. And what with Cooper being lasciviously avuncular all over her, she's in a hell of a state. She'd be fine if only she had some support.'

'She's all right with you,' said Fran.

'And with dear old Brandon,' said Mark. 'He manages to make her look like a real feisty princess.'

Libby winced at the word 'feisty' but held her tongue.

'Is there anything we can do?' asked Sir Andrew. 'I thought we could perhaps get hold of management and tell them how unprofessional we thought he was.' He turned to Libby and Fran. 'You're on the committee, aren't you? You could tell them.'

'I don't know how popular we'd be,' said Fran.

'But it's worth a try,' said Libby.

Back at Coastguard Cottage, Guy poured them all a nightcap and Fran took Libby into the kitchen for a conference.

'So, what do you think?' she said.

'I think it's a mess,' said Libby. 'But I don't see what we can do about it. Yes, we can have a word with the management team, but none of them know anything about managing a theatre, let alone a production. Andrew and Abby would carry more weight.'

'But I can see why Dame Amanda wouldn't want to put her oar in,' said Fran. 'Favouritism.'

'I suppose so,' said Libby. 'Oh, well, I'll ring the chair tomorrow. What was his name again?'

'Roland Carey. An accountant.'

'Oh, yes. He'll be a great help.'

Mr Carey, however, wasn't even in the country, preparing himself for the onslaught of the British taxation system in January by retreating to Florida for a month.

'All right for some,' said Libby, returning to the sitting room of Coastguard Cottage after her abortive phone call the following morning.

'Who's the vice-chair?' asked Guy.

'No idea,' said Fran. 'We've got a list somewhere…'

'I'll look it up when I get home,' said Libby. 'Meanwhile, I shall forget all about it for the time being. It's a Steeple Martin Sunday, and Hetty's roast awaits.'

Ben's mother Hetty still lived in The Manor, the Wilde family home, and expected her extended family to lunch every Sunday, where she provided an enormous joint of beef, mounds of perfect roast potatoes, and all the accoutrements.

Today, apart from Libby and Ben, who had brought Guy and Fran with them, Hetty's brother Lenny and his partner Flo were attending, Flo having provided the wine, being somewhat of an expert thanks to her late husband, a bit of a wine buff. They were also surprised to find Edward Hall, a historian whom Libby and Fran had managed to involve in more than one adventure so far, chatting companionably to Chief Detective Inspector Ian Connell, a family friend and firm favourite of Hetty's.

'What are you doing here?' Libby asked. 'Don't tell me you've finally found a house?'

'Soul of tact as usual, Libby,' said Ian. 'As it happens, he has.'

This surprised the entire company into silence, except for Hetty, who placidly went on pouring Yorkshire pudding mixture into baking tins.

'I'll pour the wine,' said Ben.

'No you won't,' said Flo. 'You sit down and leave it to me. Young Ian's going to explain.'

Young Ian, looking faintly disconcerted, cleared his throat.

'There's no great mystery,' he said. 'It just happened that Edward found a property and asked my opinion on it.'

'Why didn't he ask us?' demanded Libby.

'I am here, you know,' said Edward, white teeth flashing in his endearing grin. 'Ian had put me on to a previous property, so it was natural that I should ask him about this one.'

'So he came down to see it,' said Ian.

Both Edward and Ian now sat grinning smugly at the rest of the company.

'So what have you done?' asked Libby. 'Bought the Manor from under us?'

'Lovely though it is,' said Edward, 'no. Have you come across Grove House?'

Fran, Guy and Libby shook their heads.

'Isn't it somewhere near Shott? That one?' asked Ben.

'Yes,' said Edward. 'Almost within walking distance of The Poacher. You know that, don't you?'

'Oh, yes!' said Libby and Fran together.

'They always know pubs,' muttered Guy.

'Well that's it. Not all of it, of course. It was divided some years ago.'

'How did you know it was for sale?' Libby asked, turning to Ian.

'I get to hear things,' said Ian. 'So I mentioned it to Edward.'

'Did you know about this, Mum?' asked Ben.

Hetty, with a small smile, shrugged.

'Yes, she did,' said Edward. 'I came down and stayed overnight when I first viewed the property, and then again last night. I got the keys yesterday.'

'And you kept it from us!' said Libby.

Fran laughed. 'They'd never have heard the last of it if they hadn't.'

'It don't matter,' said Hetty, plonking a large dish on the table. 'Always welcome here, but it's his own business.'

Over lunch, Edward was persuaded to describe his new home, until Ian changed the subject by asking what Libby was nosing into at the moment.

'That's not very nice,' she countered.

'But you are,' said Ben. 'Although you were asked.'

Ian raised his eyebrows and looked at Fran, who sighed.

'It's true,' she said, and told him what had been going on at The Alexandria.

'At least it's unlikely to involve the police,'

said Libby, with a sniff.

After lunch, when Hetty had retired to her sitting room and Flo and Lenny had returned to Maltby Close, Ian and Edward accompanied Libby, Ben, Fran ,and Guy to the Pink Geranium, the restaurant owned by Ben's cousin Peter and Peter's partner Harry, the *chef patron*. It was traditional for them to gather at Peter and Harry's cottage on a Sunday afternoon, but this was December, and Sunday lunchtimes were busier than usual.

Harry was reclining over two chairs at the big table in the window, still wearing his whites, while Peter was fetching clean glasses and bottles from the bar area. Informed of Edward's imminent move, Peter and Harry both expressed delight, and Harry attempted to embarrass Edward by flirting with him.

'It never works, Harry,' said Edward, laughing.

'So, dear heart,' said Peter, when they were all settled with drinks - and Ian, who still had to drive back home, with coffee - 'what have you been getting up to this week? How are panto rehearsals going?'

'Fine,' said Libby, 'but the Nethergate panto is a bit of a disaster.'

Between them, Fran and Libby described the situation at The Alexandria.

Harry looked thoughtful.

'What did you say this Puss was called?'

'Ackroyd Lane, now,' said Libby.

'But I knew him as Ackroyd Lee,' said Fran. 'He was a dancer when I knew him, but that was twenty-five years ago – more, probably.'

'Only,' said Harry, sitting forward on his chair, 'I knew an Ackroyd when I first came to London.' He looked at Ian. 'You could look him up. Only he wasn't Ackroyd anything, then. He was plain old Bill Ackroyd.'

'There must be thousands of Ackroyds, though,' said Guy. 'Why should this one be the same one?'

Harry shrugged. 'Just struck a chord, that's

all.'

'But why?' asked Libby. Harry shook his head.

Ian was frowning. 'No, go on, Harry. There must have been a reason.'

'It was when I first came to London, I said.' Harry looked quickly at Peter and away again.

Peter reached out and touched his partner's arm. 'I think I know.' He caught Ian's eye, who nodded.

'I'll look him up.' He picked up his coffee cup. 'So the pantomime's carrying on, then, Libby?'

'Er – yes.' Libby looked slightly confused.

'So's ours,' said Ben, 'with all the normal problems.'

'Problems?' said Libby sharply. 'We haven't got any problems!'

Fran administered her usual kick under the table. Libby scowled.

'Well, we haven't,' she muttered.

The talk turned to other matters, then Ian got

up to leave.

'When are you moving in?' asked Ben. 'Will you want a hand? And what about you, Edward?'

'I've booked a removal company for this week,' said Edward. 'I'll let you know when.'

'So what was that all about?' said Libby to Ben, as they walked back to Allhallow's Lane. 'With Harry? Why did Fran shut me up?'

'Libby, my love,' said Ben, draping his arm round her shoulders, 'you really aren't that thick. You, of all people, should remember what Harry's told you about his life when he first went to London. He's not proud of it.'

'Oh!' Light dawned. 'You mean this Whatsisname Ackroyd was part of that scene?'

'Yes, dear.' Ben administered a congratulatory pat. 'And a not very savoury one, either, I suspect.'

'Oh, dear.' Libby bit her lip. 'It was very brave of Hal, wasn't it? He hates talking about it.'

'Exactly. So don't you go and start trying to winkle it out of him. If Ian wants to look this person up, let him and leave it at that.'

'What? You mean I can't even use it to blackmail Puss?' Libby giggled and ducked an imaginary blow. 'Come on, race you back.'

The following morning, Libby found the name and number of the vice-chair of The Alexandria Management Committee and rang her.

'Mrs Flowers? Libby Sarjeant here. As you probably know, Fran Wolfe and I accompanied Dame Amanda Knight and Sir Andrew McColl to see *Puss in Boots* on Saturday.'

'Er – yes?' Mrs Flowers sounded nervous.

'Well, I'm afraid we weren't impressed.'

'Oh, dear! But -'

'It isn't that it's a bad production, Mrs Flowers,' said Libby hastily, 'but the behaviour of one of the principals is very unprofessional and is damaging the rest of the cast.'

'Oh…' Now Mrs Flowers sounded puzzled.

'But I don't – I mean, I can't – well, I don't know anything about it.'

'No.' Libby sighed. 'But we think something needs to be said, or at least one of the cast will walk out. The director needs to put his foot down, which so far, he hasn't.'

'Oh,' said Mrs Flowers again. 'Which cast person is it?'

'Puss.'

'*Puss*?' This came out as a shriek. 'But he's the star!'

Libby rolled her eyes. 'The children think far more of young Holly, the Princess, and Mark, who plays Tom, and it's Holly Puss seems to be targeting.'

'Oh, dear! I don't know what to do! I'm afraid Roland isn't here.'

'No, we know that. But I think if you could come down to the theatre with me and Fran Wolfe – today, if possible – and have a word with the director, it would help.'

'I don't know… what time? I mean, I've

got… well, er, things to do…'

'This afternoon, sometime? Before the evening performance, anyway.'

'About five, then?' suggested Mrs Flowers.

'That's fine. I'll get hold of the director and make sure he's there. We'll meet you in the lobby, shall we? Or would you like us to pick you up?'

'No, no! It's fine. I'll see you there.' Mrs Flowers cut the connection. Libby shook her head at the phone, then rang Fran to tell her, before calling Sam the director, who gloomily assented without even asking what it was about.

At five o'clock, Libby and Fran walked down the slope to The Alexandria. Victoria Place, in honour of the season, was lit up, and the dome on top of The Alexandria was floodlit. Outside the double doors waited a small, plump woman wearing unfortunate jeans and a pink anorak.

'Mrs Flowers?' asked Libby, holding out her hand. 'I'm Libby Sarjeant.'

'And I'm Fran Wolfe.' Fran held out hers.

Mrs Flowers shook them both in an unresisting manner, and Libby pushed open the doors. Inside, they found Sam in the box office with the box office manager, both of them staring at the computer screen. He saw the deputation and reluctantly left the office.

'Sam,' Libby began, 'we on the management committee aren't very happy about some aspects of this production.'

Sam shook his head mournfully. 'Neither are we.' He looked between the three women. 'It's Puss, isn't it?'

'We were in the audience Saturday night,' Fran reminded him.

'I know.' Sam sighed. 'And you didn't stay behind afterwards.'

'Well, we were all so disappointed,' said Libby. 'And I'm afraid we reported to the rest of the management committee.' She indicated Mrs Flowers. 'Mrs Flowers is the Deputy Chair.'

'It's Puss, isn't it?' said Sam.

'Principally,' said Fran, 'although Cooper and Sheila could both do with toning down a bit. Otherwise it's a decent production. But they aren't pulling together, and certainly Mark Jones, Holly Westcott, and Clemency Knight are very unhappy.'

'I know.' Sam looked ready to break down. 'If only Ackroyd would calm down, I think the rest would be all right, but I just don't know what to do.'

'Mrs Flowers?' Libby turned to the deputy Chair, who looked horrified.

'Me? I – er -'

'Threaten him with the sack,' said Fran bluntly.

'I can't,' said Sam, equally bluntly. 'He said to me on Saturday that I couldn't sack him, or I knew what would happen.'

'And what did that mean?' asked Libby.

'I – er – don't know,' said Sam, looking furtive.

'Well,' said Libby, 'he can't threaten us, so I

suggest you ask him to come here now, and we'll threaten him. It doesn't matter what he says to us, it can't hurt us.'

'Don't you believe it,' muttered Sam. However he pulled a mobile out of his pocket and found what was presumably Ackroyd's number. After a long silent wait, he shook his head. 'Voicemail,' he said.

'What time is he supposed to be here?' asked Fran.

'Well, by the half, obviously, but he's usually early to get into costume and make-up. Usually between six and six thirty. They're all in by six thirty.'

'Clemency said he has a flat?' said Libby.

'Yes, in that converted hotel along Victoria Place. None of us have ever been there.'

'Well, he won't be en route yet,' said Fran. 'It's less than five minutes' walk.'

'Excuse me,' the box office manager called through her window, 'but if you're looking for Puss, he went up to wardrobe earlier. Said he was meeting someone who was going to mend his costume.'

'Who?' Sam was frowning.

Box Office shrugged. 'No idea.'

'How much earlier?' asked Libby.

'Just after shift change in here. Ooh, say about half two?'

'Why would he be up there all that time?' asked Sam.

'Did you know about his costume needing mending?' asked Fran.

'No. It was fine at the walk down yesterday afternoon.' He shook his head. 'But he was that fussy.'

'Did he go up the front staircase?' Libby asked Box Office, who nodded. 'Well, he could have come out the back way and gone to the dressing rooms. Perhaps he decided to stay here until the costume was ready and have a nap?'

'Shall I go up and look?' said Sam.

'Try Wardrobe first,' said Fran. 'See if his costume is really there.'

'Shall I come with you?' asked Libby.

'I'll be quicker on my own,' said Sam, and made for the ornate staircase. 'If he's not there I'll go down to the dressing rooms.'

'What about me?' A quavery voice reminded them that Mrs Flowers was still with them.

'We need you to back us up,' said Libby, wondering privately if the Deputy Chair could back anyone up.

The door at the top of the staircase crashed back on its hinges and Sam catapulted through, grasping at the gallery rail and making inarticulate noises.

Libby started running up the stairs.

'Oh, no,' muttered Fran.

'What?' whispered Mrs Flowers.

'I think this means that Puss is dead.'

Box Office was already on the phone. 'Which service?' she mouthed at Fran.

'Police and ambulance,' Fran mouthed back, and started up the stairs after Libby.

By the time she reached the top, Sam had slid to a sitting position on the gallery floor and Libby had disappeared through the door.

'Ackroyd,' muttered Sam.

'I gathered that,' said Fran. 'The police will be here soon.'

'P-p-police?'

'Yes. And ambulance.'

'B-b-but he's dead!'

'Quite,' said Fran.

Just then Libby came out of the doors looking pale. 'Throat,' she said succinctly.

'Police and ambulance are on their way,' said Fran. 'Shall we go down?'

'I'd better stay here,' said Libby. 'Can you take Sam down?'

'I'll try.' Fran looked at Sam dubiously.

'Mrs F looks a bit dodgy, too,' said Libby, peering over the gallery rail.

'You don't look so hot yourself,' muttered Fran, hauling the director to his feet. 'Come on, feller.'

Fran and Sam had barely arrived at the bottom of the staircase when the sound of sirens preceded the entry of two uniformed police officers and an ambulance crew, all of whom raced up the stairs. Libby waved them through the doors and descended herself.

Box Office, a seemingly unflappable and efficient young woman, had caused chairs to materialise, and Libby, Fran, Sam, and Mrs Flowers collapsed on to them with relief.

'Could I go home now?' asked Mrs Flowers, after a moment.

'Not until the police have spoken to us,' said Libby. 'I'm sorry we seem to have got you involved with this, but the management committee would have been anyway, even if you hadn't been here.'

Mrs Flowers glared at her. 'Why? Nothing to do with us.'

Sam, Fran, Libby, and Box Office all stared at her in amazement. Under their combined scrutiny she began to turn a pretty shade of red.

One of the policemen came down the stairs looking grim.

'Who found the body, please?'

Sam muttered a barely audible, 'I did.'

'And you are, sir?' The officer took out the inevitable notebook.

'Sam Washburn, director.'

'Director? Company director?'

'No, officer,' said Libby, 'director of the pantomime currently running in this theatre.'

'And your name, madam?' The officer fixed her with a stare.

'Mrs Libby Sarjeant,' said Libby. 'With a J.'

The officer's pencil stopped in mid-air.

'That's done it,' muttered Fran. He fastened his gimlet eye on her.

'And you, madam?'

Fran told him. He turned to Mrs Flowers.

'Jennifer Flowers. I'm nothing to do with it,' she quavered. The officer raised his eyebrows.

'Mrs Flowers,' said Libby, gazing on the pink anorak with dislike, is on the management committee of the theatre. 'Mrs Wolfe and I are consultants.'

'Mrs Sarjeant and Mrs Wolfe are well known to us, Ted.' Box Office popped her head out of her window. He turned to her in relief.

'OK, Bryony,' he said. 'Tell us what happened this afternoon.'

'Earlier on, Puss came in -'

'That was…?' Ted gestured upstairs.

'That's him. Bad mood as usual. Then, later, Mr Washburn came in. Then Mrs Sarjeant, Mrs Wolfe, and Mrs Flowers. Don't often see Mrs Flowers round here. Mr Washburn went up to see if Puss was in Wardrobe.'

'Wardrobe? Is that…?'

'Where he was found, officer, yes,' said Libby. 'Where all the costumes are kept.'

'Why did you go up there?' Officer Ted turned back to Sam.

'To look for him.'

'That's why we were here,' said Fran. 'He was going to be reprimanded.'

'Torn off a strip,' confirmed Libby, with a nod.

'So there was bad feeling?' Officer Ted's eyes lit up.

Libby sighed.

'No more than in any office,' said Fran.

The officer tucked his notebook away and glared impartially at them all.

'Wait here, please,' he said, and stamped away through the main doors.

'Phoning for assistance,' said Fran, with a sigh.

'I do not see why I have to wait here.' Mrs Flowers' voice squeaked shrilly through the foyer, and she stood up. 'I'm going home.'

'Good luck with that,' said Libby, as the little woman strode, slightly unsteadily, towards the doors. As she reached them, they swung inwards and she was nearly knocked flat on her back.

Two plain clothes officers barrelled their way through and charged up the stairs. Mrs Flowers was none too gently escorted back to her seat.

A few minutes later, one of the plain clothes officers returned and approached his witnesses. He repeated what they had told Officer Ted, took down their full names, and told the three women they could go home.

'Not you, though, sir,' said the officer with a grim smile. 'You're actually working here at the moment? We'd like you to stay.'

'Yes, well -' began Sam.

'But, officer,' said Libby, 'they need to know if they can open tonight. Sam needs to let the cast know, and if they can't open, Bryony – was it? – needs to put her plans in place to let audiences know. They're sold out, you see.'

The full horror of the situation hit everyone, especially Bryony.

'Oh, my Gawd!' she said and hurried into the box office.

The officer suddenly looked out of his depth and looked beseechingly at Libby. Surprised, she smiled at him.

'You are?' she said.

'DC Stan Bennett.' He cleared his throat. 'I worked with – ah – Inspector Maiden.'

'Did we ever meet?' Libby continued smiling.

'Er – no, ma'am. Not in person.'

'Who's the SIO this time?' she asked, aware of Sam's and Mrs Flowers' surprised stares.

'Probably DS Morgan. He's upstairs.'

'Could you ask him, then, about tonight?'

DC Bennett bobbed his head and went charging back up the stairs.

'Are you police?' asked Mrs Flowers.

'He'll get into trouble, now,' said Fran.

'No, he won't. Besides, that first officer recognised our names. He should have passed it on.'

Sam sat up straight. 'I don't understand. *Are* you police? And what's SIO?'

'No.' Fran shook her head. 'We've just had rather a lot to do with them.'

'And SIO is Senior Investigating Officer,' added Libby.

'Why couldn't you tell them to let me go, then?' said Mrs Flowers.

Libby raised her eyebrows. 'Who do you think I am? I can't tell the police what to do.'

Mrs Flowers opened her mouth, caught Fran's eye, and shut it again.

DC Bennett, followed by DS Morgan, came back down the stairs.

'I'm sorry, ladies and gentlemen,' said DS Morgan, not sounding in the least sorry, 'you won't be able to open tonight. I apologise for the inconvenience, but it's not our fault, I'm afraid.'

'No, it's bloody Puss's fault,' said Sam, glaring up the stairs.

'Hardly,' said Libby.

'It's the murderer's,' said Fran.

Sam looked somewhat abashed. 'Oh, yes. Right.'

'Is there anyone we should inform?' asked DS Morgan.

'Only the company,' said Sam. 'I'll do that, if I can use the office?'

'Where's that?' asked DC Bennett.

'There.' Sam pointed to a door under the stairs.

'It was the original office,' Libby began, 'when this was a seaside concert hall.'

'All right, Lib. They don't want to know.' Fran gave her friend a nudge. Libby went pink.

'All right, then, you can go,' said DS Morgan, 'but we will want to speak to you again. Do we have your addresses?'

Having checked the addresses, DC Bennett and DS Morgan went back up to the gallery. Mrs Flowers, without saying a word to anybody, scuttled out of the main doors, Bryony was already on the phone and Sam dived into the office. Libby and Fran followed him.

'Can we do anything?' asked Fran.

'Could you stick a few "cancelled" strips up?' asked Sam, looking woebegone.

'On the posters along the promenade?' said Libby.

'Please.' Sam fished out some pre-printed

strips and handed them over. 'We always have some, just in case.' He sighed. 'Didn't imagine quite this scenario, though.'

Libby and Fran trailed through the foyer, explained to the uniform on duty what they were doing, stuck a couple of 'cancelled' strips either side of the entrance, and plodded up to Victoria Parade. As they made their way back after papering the whole of the promenade with the depressing pieces of paper, they heard their names called out.

'Jane!' Libby turned and looked up at the thin terraced house above on Cliff Terrace.

'What's going on?' called Jane Baker from her front steps.

They crossed over and explained.

'Don't publish it yet, though,' said Fran. 'The police don't quite know how to handle it yet. They haven't appointed an SIO, even.'

Jane raised her eyebrows. 'Not even DCI Connell?'

'Not even him,' said Libby with a grin.

'Although he's supposed to be desk-bound these days.'

'That'll be the day,' said Fran. 'Anyway, Jane, we'll let you know as soon as there's anything worth saying.'

'Somebody will have let it out on social media, anyway,' said Libby, as they went back down the slope to The Alexandria. 'Bryony or someone.'

'And we're mixed up in it again,' said Fran, on a long sigh. 'How do we do it?'

Back in the office, Sam allowed them to use one of the phones to alert their loved ones and Dame Amanda and Sir Andrew of the situation. Dame Amanda agreed to let Clemency know, but sounded very shaky.

'I know he wasn't a very nice person,' said Libby, staring up at a highly coloured portrait of the founder of The Alexandria, Dorinda Castle, 'but it's a horrible thing to have happened, and just before Christmas, too.'

'She'd have known how to deal with him,'

said Fran, following Libby's eyes.

'Oh, I don't know,' said Libby. 'She had a few hairy moments, didn't she? Remember what Bella told us.'

Sam was looking interested. 'You know about the history of the place?'

'Er – yes,' said Fran, and buried her face in her large handbag.

'Is that why you're consultants?' he went on.

'In a way,' said Libby. 'And now, if there's nothing else you want us to do, we'll get out of your hair.' She stood up and smiled brightly. 'I expect we'll see you over the next few days.'

She swept out of the office, followed by Fran.

'I don't know why we're so wary of talking about the dear old place,' she said, as they walked over to the box office.

'It isn't the pleasantest story,' said Fran.

'Even if it did bring us a second theatre, in a way,' said Libby.

'And me a cat,' added Fran.

Bryony peered out of her cubbyhole.

'You off, then?'

'Yes, they've given us permission,' said Fran. 'What about you?'

'They'll let me out when I've sorted this lot. *If* I can sort it,' said Bryony gloomily.

'I wonder what they'll do about Puss?' said Libby. 'Do you think the understudy's strong enough?'

Bryony shrugged. 'No idea.'

'Do you realise,' said Fran ten minutes later, as they walked along Harbour Street towards Coastguard Cottage, 'we haven't once wondered who did it.'

Libby stopped dead. 'Good Lord,' she said. 'So we haven't.'

'Well,' said Fran, starting to walk again, 'there appears to be a choice. So many people didn't like him.'

'But not enough to kill him,' said Libby.

'We don't know that,' said Fran. 'Anyway, someone did.'

Libby nodded soberly. 'Unless it was an accident.'

Fran gave her a look. 'You said it was his throat. How can that be an accident?'

'Oh, well.' Libby looked sideways. 'You know…'

'No, I don't.' Fran took out her key. 'Are you coming in?'

'I suppose I ought to go home, really. Ben'll want to know what's happened.'

'OK. Will you ring if you hear anything?'

'Yes – and you will, too, won't you?' Libby sighed and shook her head. 'Poor things. Their first panto and this has to happen.'

Ben had his own news to impart when Libby arrived, having helped Edward move the first of his possessions into his new flat.

'It's lovely, Lib.' He handed her a whisky and poked up the fire. 'It's a perfect little white Georgian house, and it's been divided really well. Edward has the ground floor and the main entrance, and the upper floor is reached from the back, but the two are completely separate. Now tell me what's been going on at The Alexandria.'

Libby told him.

'So it looks as if people were right about him being a nasty piece of work,' he said thoughtfully when she'd finished.

'It doesn't always follow that just because someone's murdered they were a nasty piece of work,' said Libby.

'No, but in this case it looks like it, doesn't it?' Ben sipped his whisky. 'I wonder if Ian had any luck looking him up?'

'No idea. Should we ask, do you think? Will he want to know?'

'I think it would be rather odd if we didn't tell him,' said Ben. 'A murder on his own doorstep?'

'I suppose so,' said Libby, 'but he probably knows already.'

'It won't be his baby, though, will it?'

'I wouldn't have thought so.' Libby drew up

her knees and hugged them. 'So we can speculate to our heart's content.'

There was a knock on the door.

'Oh,' said Ben, 'I forgot to tell you.'

'Tell me what?' said Libby, suspiciously.

'Harry's trying out a new recipe on us.' Ben grinned over his shoulder. 'I said you'd be delighted.'

Harry came in and went straight through to the kitchen bearing a large enamel dish. Peter came in and put down two bottles of red wine.

'If you're forced to eat Hal's experiments,' he said, 'the least we can do is provide something to wash them down with.'

The "experiment" turned out to be red lentil meatballs in a vegetarian sauce with egg-free tagliatelle.

'There are times,' said Libby with her mouth full, 'when I could easily become a veggie.'

'Only because I treat you so well,' said Harry. 'And now, petal, you are going to tell us just what's been going on down in Nethergate.

You muttered something about Puss Ackroyd as we came in.'

Libby sat back in her chair and sighed. 'He's dead,' she said.

'*Dead*?' Harry's mouth fell open.

'Murdered, apparently,' said Ben. 'Throat -'

'All right!' interposed Libby sharply. 'We went to give him a ticking off, along with the director and the deputy chair of the Alexandria trust. The director found him in the Wardrobe.'

'Not a lion and witch sort of wardrobe, I take it,' said Peter.

'No.' Libby shook her head and forked up some more tagliatelle. 'In amongst the costumes. He'd gone to have his mended.'

'Have you told Ian?' Harry had put his fork down and was staring intently at Libby.

'No – it isn't his case. He'll have heard about it anyway.'

'You need to tell him.'

'Why?'

Harry gave the impression of gritting his

teeth. 'He was going to look your Ackroyd Lane up.'

'Ian thought there was something wrong about him, too.' Peter confirmed.

'In that case,' said Ben, 'I wouldn't mind betting that we don't have to bother about letting him know. He'll come to us. Or to Fran.'

Libby scraped up the last of her sauce. 'Why don't you tell us about the Ackroyd you knew in London?' she said to Harry.

He pushed his plate away. 'Did you like the meatballs?'

'Yes, I've already said.' Libby glared at him.

'Go on, love,' said Peter. 'It'll come out now, anyway, if it *is* him.'

'I looked him up,' said Harry. 'It is.' He stared at his plate for a few moments, then looked up at Libby and gave a crooked smile. 'Do you remember sitting out on that terrace thing on the Isle of Wight?'

'I'll never forget it.'

'And I told you all about the children's

homes and the club?'

'Yes.'

'Well, Puss Ackroyd worked at the club, too.'

Ben and Libby gasped.

'Yes. He was scraping around trying to get chorus jobs in those days.'

'Fran said he was chorus when she knew him.'

'Well, at this time he was plain Bill Ackroyd, and he just loved little boys.' Harry made a face. 'After one incident too many, Pierre – the chef – chucked him out. And he threatened Pierre, tried to intimidate some of the staff, and, in the end, had a go at me. This wasn't long before Pete rescued me.'

'So did Ian find anything about him?' asked Ben.

'Give the bloke a chance!' said Harry. 'This was only yesterday.'

Libby pushed her chair back. 'Does anyone want coffee?'

'No, more wine, please,' said Harry. He stood

up. 'I'm traumatised.'

Peter gave him a friendly buffet on the arm and they trooped into the sitting room. They had barely sat down when another knock sounded on the front door.

'Guess who,' said Ben.

Ian Connell walked into the sitting room and shook his head.

'I might have known.'

'No, you mightn't,' said Libby. 'Harry came round to try out a new recipe on us.'

'And you didn't even mention the murder that happened at The Alexandria today?'

'I asked her,' said Harry. 'Sit down, Ian.' Harry himself slid to the floor and leant against Peter's chair. Ian looked at Ben for guidance, then sat down.

'What do you want?' asked Libby. 'It isn't your case, is it?'

'Strictly, no.' Ian eyed the wine glasses.

'No, you can't have wine if you're driving home,' said Libby.

'I'll make you coffee,' said Ben, and vanished into the kitchen.

'I got in touch with Nethergate as soon as we heard,' said Ian. 'I'd found out a little about Bill Ackroyd, you see.'

'Puss's real name,' said Libby.

Ben came in with the cafetière, a mug and milk jug on a tray.

'What were you saying?' He sat down on the sofa next to Libby.

'Bill, as Hal remembered him,' said Ian, 'was born William Ackroyd. Where the Lane came from, heaven knows. As William Ackroyd, he had convictions, and had also appeared in pantomime several times.'

'He had?' Libby's eyebrows rose. 'As a principal, or chorus?'

'Chorus. In *Cinderella*. And Cinderella was Sheila Bernard.'

'Really? So he could have claimed to have something on her, too?' said Libby.

'If that's what he was doing, yes.'

'That's what Mark and Clemency thought.'

'Are they an item?' asked Harry.

'I don't think so. I think Mark's more interested in young Holly.'

Harry wrinkled his nose.

'I'm sure she's very nice,' said Libby with a sniff.

'Do you mind telling me what happened today?' asked Ian, accepting a mug from Ben.

'Go on, petal,' said Harry.

'We don't mind hearing it again,' said Peter with a wry grin.

'Well,' said Libby, looking at Ben. 'I suppose…'

She related the story of Ackroyd's abortive telling off and its aftermath.

'Hmm,' said Ian when she'd finished. 'And this Sam was in the theatre when you arrived?'

'Yes, but…' Libby's eyes widened in alarm. 'It wasn't him! He'd only arrived half an hour before us.'

'And when did Lane arrive?'

'Half two, according to Box Office.'

'Box Office?'

'The box office manager. Bryony Nice girl. She's been there for a couple of years, now.'

'Do you know who's in charge down there?' asked Harry.

'The SIO? No,' said Ian. 'I shall get hold of him tomorrow, though. I think he probably needs to know what I've found out.'

'Surely he'd find that out himself?' said Ben. 'Or his team would.'

'Not necessarily right back to the Bill Ackroyd days,' said Ian.

'What were the offences?' asked Libby.

'That's under wraps at the moment, I'm afraid,' said Ian, and glanced at Harry, who shook his head.

'Did any of the other names come up?'

'I don't know all of the other names,' said Ian evasively.

'That probably means they did,' said Libby.

Ian laughed. 'How you do jump to

conclusions!'

He drank the rest of his coffee and stood up. 'I'll keep you informed as far as I'm able,' he said. 'And of course, it goes without saying that you'll tell me if you hear anything, won't you?'

He gazed round at the four innocent faces looking up at him and sighed. Ben grinned and stood up to see him out.

'By the way,' he said, 'I helped Edward move into Grove House today. Lovely place.'

Ian half turned in the doorway. 'I didn't know he was moving today.'

'Not completely,' said Ben. 'He's going back up to – Leicester, was it? – tonight to collect some furniture. I expect he'll spend the rest of the week moving in.'

'Hmm,' said Ian. 'I'll see if he wants a hand.'

'Now why,' said Libby, after Ben had shut the door, 'didn't he seem pleased about Ben helping Edward?'

'Or was it,' said Harry, 'that he didn't know Edward was moving this week? That's what he said.'

'But still – why?' Libby frowned. 'And why didn't we know they'd become such good friends?'

Peter smiled. 'And they looked at each other with such a wild surmise.'

'It's not that,' said Harry. 'My gaydar has never gone off near Ian or Edward.'

'And remember Ian and Fran,' said Libby.

'Maybe we'll get to know Ian a little better through Edward,' said Ben comfortably. 'Now, any more wine for anyone?'

As soon as Ben had left for his distillery on Tuesday morning, Libby called Fran.

'It's all right, I know,' said Fran.

'What do you know? You don't know what I was going to say.'

'That Ian came round to see you last night.'

'Oh. Yes.'

'He called this morning.'

'Oh!' Libby frowned at Sidney, who was

twining hopefully round her ankles. 'He didn't call me.'

'He wanted to tell me what he told you last night, and to say an officer would be round to take a statement later this morning, and if you were here, you could give yours at the same time.'

'Cheek!' said Libby.

Fran laughed. 'No, why? Because he knows us so well? Anyway, are you coming down? Clemency rang as well. She'd like to talk to us, too.'

'Oh, OK. I must get back at a reasonable time, though. I've got panto rehearsal tonight and we've got a costume fitting going on at the same time.'

'Rather you than me,' said Fran. 'I'll see you in – what? An hour?'

'Ish,' said Libby. 'I'm not dressed yet.'

In fact, it was after 11 o'clock when Libby arrived at Coastguard Cottage, to find Clemency already sitting in front of the woodburner in the sitting room looking miserable.

'What's been going on, then?' asked Libby, shrugging off her new cape. 'Are they letting you open today?'

'No,' said Fran, as Clemency shook her head. 'And it looks as though Ian's butted in and made himself SIO.'

'Oh, dear. That won't make him popular.'

'You wouldn't have thought so, but it appears that they actually *asked* him.'

'They did?' Libby's eyebrows shot up. 'Why?'

'Because he has experience with what DS Morgan called "these sort of cases",' said Fran. 'He told Clemency.'

'They've been to see you, have they?' Libby turned to the younger woman. 'What did they say?'

'She was just telling me,' said Fran. 'Give her a chance.'

'Bryony called us all yesterday late afternoon

to tell us what had happened, but Cooper wasn't satisfied and turned up at the theatre. They practically arrested him on the spot, according to him.' Clemency gave a nervous little laugh. 'He phoned us all when they let him go, trying to get sympathy, I think. Anyway, he said he doubted they'd let us go on today, and he was right. DS Morgan came to see me earlier – about nine, it was.'

'What did he ask?'

'Had I known Ackroyd before this panto, mainly. And where was I yesterday. I told him what Ackroyd had said about me getting the part and what we thought he probably said to everyone else. And then he asked to speak to Mum.'

'Did he?' Fran looked startled. 'Why?'

'Because he accused me of getting the part through her, I suppose.' Clemency's brow wrinkled. 'They sent me out of the room, and Mum wouldn't tell me afterwards. It was scary.'

There was a sharp knock on the front door.

'That'll be the police now,' said Libby. 'You'd better go in the kitchen, Clemmie.'

Fran opened the door to disclose DC Bennett on the step, looking sheepish.

'Mrs Wolfe,' he said, bobbing his head. 'All right if I come in?'

He stopped dead when he saw Clemency about to enter the kitchen.

'I take it DCI Connell sent you to take statements from Mrs Wolfe and me?' said Libby, taking the bull by the horns. 'Miss Knight was just telling us about her own interview, but she'll go into the kitchen while you talk to us.'

DC Bennett's mouth closed with a snap.

'Do sit down, officer,' said Fran, smiling kindly. 'A lot of work for you, I imagine, a case like this. Not easy, just before Christmas.'

'Er – no, ma'am.' DC Bennett perched on the edge of one of Fran's beautiful button-back chairs and took out a tablet.

'High tech today?' said Libby. 'Easier to

share information, I suppose.'

'Er – yes.' DC Bennett cleared his throat. 'If I could just ask you to tell me what you did yesterday afternoon? You first, Mrs Wolfe.'

Patiently, Fran took him through the whole afternoon in painstaking detail. Then Libby recapped the lot.

'And you didn't know any of the cast of the pantomime before the – um – production?'

'Yes, we did. We knew Clemency Knight. She's a family friend,' said Fran. 'That's why she's here today.'

'But not Ackroyd Lane?'

'Well,' said Fran, 'I had actually met him before.'

Bennett practically fell off the chair. 'When?'

'I can't remember exactly, but it must be at least twenty-five years ago.'

'Twenty-five…'

'Yes, sorry. He wasn't known as Ackroyd Lane in those days. But you can ask DCI Connell about that. He knows all about it.'

After a moment's thought, Bennett asked a couple more desultory questions, then left.

Clemency came out of the kitchen. 'Does your DCI really know about Ackroyd?' she said.

'Yes,' said Libby. 'And in fact, another friend of ours knew him in his really early days. It's not a pretty tale.'

'Are you going to meet up with the others today?' asked Fran hastily, guessing that Libby was about to spill the Bill Ackroyd story.

'Yes. Cooper wanted us all to go out to where they're staying, but we voted for The Swan.'

'Good for you! Did he complain?'

'Apparently, yes.' Clemency grinned. 'But Sam told him we were all meeting in The Swan, and he could come if he wanted or not – just as he liked. He's coming.'

'Do you want us there?' asked Libby.

'Sam did ask me to ask you. He said, as you were there yesterday...'

'What time?' asked Fran.

'Half past twelve. I think he's managed to get

a private room.'

Clemency left and Fran and Libby sat looking at one another.

'What are we supposed to do?' said Libby.

'Provide moral support,' said Fran. 'Nothing else we can do.'

'Have you got any ideas?'

'What? About who did it? No, of course not.'

Libby got up and wandered to the window. 'I thought you might have. Who are the suspects?'

'Heavens, I don't know! The cast, I suppose.'

'And the crew? He might just as well have known the crew back in the day as the actors.'

'You can ask them, then,' said Fran. 'Shall we have some lunch before we go?'

The Swan wasn't terribly busy. Clemency was waiting with Sam in the main bar area, and smiled with relief as Libby and Fran came in.

'We're in a room back there,' said Sam, waving a vague hand. 'I'm so pleased you've come.'

'Er – yes.' Libby smiled back. 'Shall we go in?'

The last to arrive was, predictably, Cooper Fallon, followed by a timid Holly Westcott. Once everyone was seated, Sam tapped the table and cleared his throat.

'We just thought we ought to get together, to see – er – where we – um – stand.'

'What's the position taken by management?' Cooper Fallon looked at Libby and Fran. 'Presumably you can tell us?'

Fran opened her mouth and shut it again. Libby took a deep breath.

'There is no position as such. The police do not want the show going ahead until they've completed their enquiries. There is nothing management or cast can do about it. They will let us know when they consider it safe to let us go ahead.'

'Safe! That's preposterous!' Cooper burst out. 'What about our contracts?'

'Contracts?' Libby raised what she hoped

were supercilious eyebrows. 'Contracts tend not to include clauses about murder.'

There were a few sniggers and Cooper glared round at the company.

'Mrs Sarjeant and Mrs Wolfe have had experience with this sort of thing before,' said Sam. 'I suggest they tell us what they think.'

Fran looked horrified.

Clemency stood up. 'I think you all know who my mother is, and what Ackroyd had to say about that, but what I can tell you is that Fran and Libby – Mrs Wolfe and Mrs Sarjeant – helped her a great deal in similar circumstances a few years ago. At least they could tell us what to expect.'

They were a few 'hear, hears' and other murmurs of encouragement, although Cooper Fallon didn't appear enthusiastic.

'You tell 'em,' whispered Fran.

Libby stood up and smiled at Clemency.

'Thank you, Clemmie,' she said. 'Now, the main thing I can tell you – from experience – is that if you try and conceal anything from the police they will inevitably find it out, and the fact of concealing it will make the whole investigative process far more difficult, and may, in fact, get you into trouble.'

'What happens next?' asked the squeaky-voiced chorus member. 'Will they come and see us?'

'If they haven't done already,' said Libby. 'Who has spoken to the police?'

'Me,' said Sam.

'And me,' said Clemency.

'I have,' said Brandon.

'So have I,' said Mark.

'And me,' said Sheila.

'So the only two who haven't are Holly and Cooper?' said Libby. 'What about chorus and crew?'

Most of the chorus had been interviewed together in their boarding house by Bennett and Morgan, and some of the technical crew who lived locally.

'We didn't know him, though,' said a large, balding man wearing a thick fleece. 'We're local. He wasn't. Unpleasant git, by all accounts, though.'

'Pain in the neck to work with,' said another, a small, wiry man with hunched shoulders. 'Never kept to his mark.'

'You Lighting?' asked Libby.

'Follow spot, yeah.' He shook his head. 'He darted in and out and then shouted at us because he couldn't find his light.'

There were more murmurs of agreement.

'And did you tell the police this?' asked Fran.

'Well, no.' The two crew members looked at one another. 'We didn't think they'd understand.'

Libby sighed. 'You must. How will they know what sort of person he was unless they hear all of this?'

They looked uncomfortable.

'Right, anything else anyone want to tell either us or the police? We'll pass it on, but you must realise that if the police think it's significant, they'll want to speak to you about it.' Libby sat down and looked round at the company.

Cooper was still huffing to himself. Holly had gone to sit next to Mark Jones, whose arm rested along the back of her chair. She tentatively raised her arm.

'He wasn't very kind,' she said quietly.

'No.' Libby smiled at her, and the rest of the company made encouraging noises.

'He was bloody awful,' said Mark. 'The things he said to Holly.'

'The things he said to all of us,' said Sheila. 'He was a bastard.'

'OK,' said Libby. 'What exactly *did* he say? And was it in the hearing of others?'

'Mostly not,' said old Brandon, in his deep rumbling voice. 'I think you've heard – and seen – some of the things he got up to…'

'That was why we were going to speak to him yesterday,' said Sam.

'But the police won't understand how awful his tricks were,' said Libby.

'They will want to know personal threats, if there are any,' said Fran. 'Were there?'

There was a good deal of glancing out of the corners of eyes and shuffling feet.

Libby gave an exasperated sigh.

'Look, you don't have to tell us here and now, but you really must tell the police when they ask,' she said.

Brandon stood up. 'I'd rather tell you,' he said. 'You can tell the police.'

'The same thing I said earlier holds good,' said Libby. 'They would still want to speak to you themselves.'

'I don't see why,' Sheila rasped out. 'I keep myself to myself.'

'Hmm,' said Fran under her breath.

'If they want to speak to me they can make an appointment,' said Cooper, loftily.

'I don't think it works like that,' said Libby gently.

Cooper made a dismissive sound and threw himself against the back of his chair.

'Well,' said Sam, 'I suggest if anyone's got anything they feel might interest the police they tell Fran and Libby and see what they think.' He looked round at his company and shrugged.

'They won't,' said Fran quietly. 'They're all scared.'

Cooper stood up. 'I'm going for lunch,' he said. 'I take it this is on expenses?'

Sam looked shocked. 'I – um – I don't think…'

Cooper glared. 'Well, I'm going. Coming, Holly?'

'N-no, thanks.' Holly gave him a frightened look and moved closer to Mark. The rest of the company began to move. Libby and Fran stayed where they were, until nearly everyone had left the room.

'Told you,' said Fran. 'It was a good idea, Sam, but they won't.'

'I will.' Brandon moved up to a chair at their

table. 'I don't know if it'll be any use, but I can't keep quiet.'

Sam, Clemency, Fran and Libby looked at him in surprise. Sam shifted in his seat.

'If you'd rather we went…' he began.

'No, stay.' Brandon sighed heavily. 'I'd rather get it off my chest. After all, anyone could have heard the poisonous little remarks that prat made. I certainly heard some of the things he said to other people. He wasn't exactly confidential about it.'

'I told you,' said Clemency. 'And they all knew what he thought about me.'

Brandon leant over and patted her arm. 'My dear Clemmie,' he said, 'you're an actor to your fingertips, mother or no mother. I've known you a good long time, after all.'

Clemency blushed.

'No, mine was far more shameful.' Brandon sighed again. 'Or at least, it was. I started in the early sixties, you see.'

'Ah,' said Libby. Brandon gave her a tight

94

little smile.

'Yes, my dear. I was "one of those", as we were called then.'

'But…' began Sam again.

Libby turned on him.

'Look, it's no good saying "but that doesn't matter now". It did then.' She turned back to Brandon.

'Well, you've guessed, haven't you? I got into trouble. And no, Sam, it doesn't matter now, although I've lost the taste for it nowadays. But it got me the sack back in the sixties and there was a time I thought I'd never work again - though thanks to a friend of yours,' he bowed towards Fran and Libby, 'I did. But little Bill just loved to remind me.'

'Bill?' said Sam.

'Andrew?' said Fran and Libby together.

'Yes, Andrew,' said Brandon. 'And Bill – that was Ackroyd Lane's real name.'

'Yes, we knew that,' said Libby, 'and I think, so would Andrew.'

'I don't understand this,' said Sam. 'Why would it matter?'

'Old scandal,' said Fran. 'He was an unpleasant little tyke, wasn't he?'

'What about the others?' asked Libby. 'You said you heard what he said about the others.'

'Their stories, dear,' said Brandon. 'I don't tell tales out of school.' He stood up and smiled at his little audience. 'Do tell your police friends, won't you?'

'Well,' said Libby, when Brandon had made his stately way out of the room. 'What do we think?'

Clemency looked uncomfortable. 'I think I sort of knew that,' she said. 'And I did tell you – well, Mark and I did – that his favourite trick was his sly little comments about things in the past. That's obviously what he was doing with Brandon.'

'And who else, do you think?' asked Fran.

'Oh, I couldn't -'

'I could,' said Sam, sitting up straight in his

chair. 'He tried it on me.'

'You?' said three voices together.

'Yes, me. Your lovely mum knows,' he said to Clemency.

'Oh, yes,' said Libby, remembering Coolidge's 'lame duck' remark.

'But what I did,' said Sam, cheeks glowing a Father Christmas red, 'was *actually* criminal.'

'So is molesting underage children,' said Libby.

'Er - yes,' said Sam, looking surprised. 'What I meant was…' he swallowed. 'I – um – misappropriated funds.' He lowered his eyes and looked miserable.

For a moment there was silence.

'And what did Ackroyd say he would do?' asked Fran gently.

'Tell management. And the cast.' Sam looked almost about to cry.

Clemency suddenly leant forward and kissed his cheek. 'If Mum knew, then management did, probably. It wasn't kept completely quiet, was it?'

'Well, no, but I didn't work for a few years.'

'And now that's over. I bet it wouldn't have made any difference,' said Clemency.

'She's right, you know,' said Libby. 'Brace up, Sam. And tell us what else he was doing.'

Sam looked round at the three women and smiled a little tremulously. 'Thank you,' he said, then cleared his throat and sat up straight. 'Anyway, he kept dropping hints about other members of the cast, suggesting they weren't good enough and had disreputable pasts. Brandon was one, Sheila was another, and Cooper was the one he was most – I don't know – gleeful about.'

'Good heavens!' said Fran. 'What had he done?'

'According to Ackroyd, what *hadn't* he done.' Sam looked gloomy.

'I think *I* know,' said Clemency, going rather pink. 'Young girls, mainly.'

'Ah,' said Fran and Libby.

'And Sheila – well, he only hinted at that, but it was something way back, you know? When she did all those leads in musicals.' Sam sighed. 'I'd better tell the police, hadn't I?'

'Let us drop a hint first,' said Libby. 'Then, if they think it's all just hearsay you won't have to say anything.'

'And precisely,' said Fran, as they walked back to Coastguard Cottage, 'how do we do that? We don't know the police team here.'

'We can text Ian,' said Libby. 'Then he can tell us what to do. You can text him.'

'Why me?'

'Because of his soft spot for you.' Libby smirked. 'Go on. Dare you.'

'Let me get indoors first,' said Fran irritably. 'And you can put the kettle on.'

Fran sent her text, Libby made the tea, and they sat and looked at one another.

'What do we think?' said Libby eventually.

'No one was very keen to talk to us, were they?' said Fran.

'As you said, they're scared.'

'But I think they all had something to say.'

'I don't often have insights,' said Libby, 'but even I felt that, too.'

Fran grinned. 'There's a breakthrough!'

'What should we do, though? Should we try and talk to them again?'

'Oh, I don't think so,' said Fran. 'They'd only clam up.'

'These two might not,' said Libby, nodding towards the window.

'Oh!' Fran stood up. 'Do we let them in?'

'Of course.' Libby beat her to the door. 'Pinch and Punch! Do come in.'

The two men, more tired-looking and older than they appeared on the stage, stepped hesitantly over the threshold.

'Sit down,' said Fran. 'Would you like tea?'

'No thanks,' said Punch. 'We had a pint in the pub.'

'We went back to see if you were still with Sam,' said Pinch, when they were seated, 'but you weren't.'

'Sam said you were going to drop a hint to the police for him,' said Punch. 'So we thought…'

'You want us to do the same for you?' said Libby.

'Well…' Pinch looked at Punch.

'We don't want to tell tales,' said Punch, 'but Ackroyd was always making snide remarks.'

'And you thought they might mean something?' suggested Fran.

They both nodded, looking uncomfortable.

'What are your real names?' asked Libby suddenly. 'We can't go on calling you Pinch and Punch.'

'Joe King,' said Pinch with a grin.

'And John Collins, would you believe,' said Punch.

'Therefore – King and Collins,' they said together.

'But he didn't have anything on us,' said Joe King. 'Although he did used to hint that we were a gay couple.'

'Which didn't worry us,' said John. 'It was other people he used to get at.'

'So we gather,' said Fran.

'He'd say things like, "The things I could tell you," or just give someone a look,' said Joe. 'Like a warning.'

'And say things,' said John. 'What was that thing he was always saying, Joe?'

'Eh? What?'

'Some American expression.' John frowned. 'Oh, you remember. Old-fashioned.'

'I don't,' said Joe.

'Nix! That was it. As though it was meant to shock.' John looked puzzled. 'It didn't fit, somehow.'

Fran looked thoughtful. 'Perhaps it *did* mean something.'

'I don't see what,' said Libby.

'Well, neither do I, yet.' Fran smiled at the two men. 'So what else?'

They fidgeted and looked at each other.

'Well, it sounds silly, now…' said John.

'But he said…' Joe looked at his friend again, 'he said he could bring the whole production down.'

Libby gasped.

'What did he mean?' asked Fran.

'We don't know. But he mentioned Clem,' said John.

'*Clemency*?' said Fran and Libby.

'That's what he said. But how could Clem bring the production down?' said Joe. 'She's the nicest…'

'She is,' said Libby. 'We've known her for some time.'

'I think it's rubbish,' said Fran. 'He was just trying to seem important.'

'That's what we thought. But now…' said John.

'You were right to tell us without the others knowing,' said Fran. 'We'll pass it on.'

'Tell me,' said Libby, 'if you're given the chance to carry on, would you want to?'

'Yes!' they said together.

'It's actually a nice little production,' said John, pursing his lips judicially. 'If you get rid of the temperaments. Holly would be just right as the Princess, Mark's a great Tom, and even Cooper's a reasonable King – just the right touch of pomposity…'

'You can say that again,' said Libby.

'What about Sheila?' asked Fran.

'Well…' said Joe.

'Her understudy's great. Girl named Honor,' said John.

'Hmm.' Libby thought for a moment. 'Well, we'll pass it all on, as we said, but I don't know what will come of it.'

Joe stood up. 'It doesn't seem much now we've brought it all out in the open.'

'But I'm glad we did,' said John, also standing up. 'Sorry we bothered you.'

"I'm not sure that got us any further forward,' said Fran, shutting the door after their guests had gone.

'All we can do is pass all that on to Ian or his minions,' said Libby, 'but they were right. It doesn't seem much.'

'Do you want any more tea?' asked Fran.

'No, I'd better get off. I've got to try and think about my panto – if I can.'

'With any luck we won't have to get involved any more with this one,' said Fran.

Libby stared out of the window at the darkening sky. 'Who do you think did it?'

Fran joined her at the window. 'I can't honestly see any of them doing it. Do you think it could have been an accident?'

'With a cut throat?' said Libby. 'Can't see it.'

'We don't even know who was in the theatre that afternoon.'

'We could ask.' Libby looked at her friend. 'If Box Office Bryony is in the theatre. She might be, to field enquiries.'

'Now?'

'Why not? Send Ian another text to tell him we've got a bit more info and we're going to check it at the theatre.'

'He'll be furious.'

'He always is,' said Libby. 'Come on.'

But when they arrived, the main doors were locked.

'Stage door?' suggested Libby.

Unwillingly, Fran followed her round the building, where, sure enough, the stage door was unlocked.

The silence of the theatre enfolded them. Libby found the light switch and they made their way to the stage. The strange whispering that always seemed to fill an empty stage sounded strange and unfamiliar, and Libby hurried to the steps that led down from the stage.

'Come on – foyer,' she said.

They crept through the dark stalls and finally emerged into the comparative brightness of the foyer, but the box office, too, was locked.

'Who's in here, then?' asked Fran. 'Someone must be.'

'Dressing rooms?' said Libby. They looked at

each other.

'Wardrobe?' said Fran.

'Let's sit down and think about this,' said Libby. 'Who might it be?'

'Techies?' Fran sat on one of the gilt chairs that stood around the foyer.

'Building manager?' Libby followed suit.

'Not necessarily the murderer.'

They both stopped and listened. Nothing.

'If it's the murderer, who? Someone who was in the pub at lunchtime,' said Fran.

'They were all there.'

'Brandon?'

'No.' They both shook their heads.

'Not Clemency.'

'No. Tom and Joe – definitely not.'

'Holly? Mark?'

They shook their heads again.

'Cooper.' Fran raised an eyebrow.

'He's nasty enough,' said Libby. 'And more worried about his career than the others.'

And as if the very sound of his name had

conjured him up, Cooper appeared at the top of the stairs.

He stopped dead. The three of them looked at one another for a long moment.

'Well, well, well.' He began to descend. 'And how are you, my lovelies? Still doing the police's work for them?'

Libby cleared her throat. 'No – we just needed a word with Box Office. But she isn't here.'

'Well, of course not. We're closed.' He arrived in front of them. 'How did you get in?'

'Stage door was unlocked,' said Fran. 'Was that you?'

Cooper looked slightly disconcerted. 'Er – yes.'

'You've got keys?' Libby was surprised.

'Yes.' He lifted his chin. 'I like access to the theatre.'

'Hmmm,' said Fran. 'Why were you in Wardrobe?'

'I wasn't!'

'That's where you were coming from,' said Libby.

The dead silence surrounded them again.

'I was looking for something.' Cooper looked a little shamefaced. 'But Wardrobe's still locked. They've got that tape over it.'

'In that case,' said Libby, standing up, 'as we've all been thwarted, I think we all ought to get out.'

Looking relieved, Cooper held open the auditorium door. 'After you.'

Nervously, Fran and Libby preceded him.

They were halfway down the aisle when they heard the noise.

'What's that?' Cooper whispered.

'Nix,' said Libby, and wondered why she'd said it. Neither of her companions reacted.

'Someone's backstage,' whispered Fran.

'Get behind me,' growled Cooper, and pushed past them. Fran and Libby exchanged surprised glances. He strode towards the stage and hopped nimbly up the steps.

'Who's there?' he called.

'*Look out!*' shouted Fran as a huge section of castle-painted scenery began to topple towards them. They all scooted into the wings and Libby took out her phone with a shaking hand.

'You all right, girls?' Cooper's voice was shaking, too.

'Dusty!' said Fran, coughing.

'Police,' Libby was saying. 'The Alexandria theatre in Nethergate. There was a murder here… yes, yes. At the moment…'

She rang off. 'They'll be here in a minute. Where did they go?'

'Our jolly attacker?' said Cooper, no longer attempting to keep his voice down, and oddly, sounding far more normal.

'Did you leave everyone in the pub?' asked Fran.

'I had lunch. I don't know where the rest went.' He peeped out on to the stage. 'Should we try and get to the stage door?'

'No, let's stay here until we hear the police,'

said Libby.

'Why did you say "Nix" out there?' Cooper looked at Libby. 'I only ask because it's an odd word to hear, and bloody Ackroyd was using it all the time.'

'That's why,' said Libby. 'I was hoping to get a reaction.'

'From me?' Cooper sounded astonished.

'From anybody. Listen.'

The faint sound of sirens was now heard, followed very quickly by heavy footsteps.

'Police!' shouted a voice.

Slowly, Cooper, Fran, and Libby emerged.

As Libby opened her mouth to explain, there was a rush of noise from the stage door and DCI Ian Connell erupted on to the stage.

'Told you he'd be furious,' muttered Fran.

'What do you think you're doing?' he yelled. Even the uniformed officers quailed.

'We – er – wanted to ask Bryony, Box Office…' began Fran.

'I wanted to find…' began Cooper.

Ian rounded on the uniformed officers. 'Why wasn't a watch kept on this building?'

'I don't think it's their case, Ian,' said Libby.

'No.' He turned back and seemed to take hold of himself. Cooper looked shell-shocked. 'Search the building, please.' He pulled out his phone and spoke urgently into it. Then came towards the dusty trio and stood looking at them with his hands on his hips. 'And now?'

Gradually, Fran and Libby told him all the titbits of information they'd gleaned, and Cooper admitted to doing a little sleuthing on his own.

'And then Mrs – er – Libby, said Nix. And I wondered why. Ackroyd was always saying it, and -'

'Nix?' Ian's voice sharpened. 'Another hint Lane was dropping?'

'We don't know.' Libby, Fran and Cooper looked at each other in puzzlement.

'Oh, I think I do.'

'Go on, then,' said Libby. 'It means nothing,

doesn't it?'

'Not exactly.' Ian let out a gusty breath. 'The Nyxes – taken from the Greek – were the names given to a group of young girls recruited back in the late eighties and nineties, let's say for immoral purposes.'

'God, yes!' exploded Cooper. 'I remember now! It was quite the scandal – provincial theatres, mainly, wasn't it?'

Ian nodded. 'Which means he thought someone in your company had been connected -' he paused, as a scuffle made itself heard somewhere on the other side of the stage. 'And he was right.'

And from the opposite wing space emerged two ruffled-looking policemen, hauling between them an equally ruffled Sheila Bernard.

Ben and Libby headed for the Pink Geranium through the silence of a winter evening. The clear sky already showed myriad stars, which were reflected in the sparkling of the frosted pavements.

'Nearly Christmas,' sighed Libby. She had missed the panto rehearsal, leaving Peter to knock her cast into submission.

Ben kissed her cold cheek. 'Nearly Christmas,' he agreed.

'So tell us the whole story,' said Harry, when Libby and Ben, together with Fran and Guy who had been invited along for support, were settled in their usual seats at the Pink Geranium.

'Well, it was as we all thought,' said Fran. 'Ackroyd had lost his telly show due to allegations of misconduct, but it hadn't been serious enough to make a big thing of it.'

'Should have been,' said Libby with a sniff.

'Anyway,' Fran went on, 'he was jealous of everyone else and spent most of his time trying to unsettle them all.'

'Trouble was, Sheila really had been involved in this whole Nyxes thing, and had escaped prosecution. No idea how, as she fairly ran the thing! She toured the provincial theatres back in those days - very handy for recruiting young girls. She thought he knew all, as they say,' said Libby. 'So, as far as we can make out, she went to try and talk to him, saying she'd help with his costume. She was a dab hand, apparently.'

'How did she get in and out without being seen?' asked Ben.

'She'd long gone by the time we got there,' said Fran. 'Through the stage door. It really should be secured properly. We'll have to bring that up at committee.'

'She kept saying it was an accident,' said Libby.

'Throat cut?' said Harry disbelievingly.

'That's what I said,' said Libby. 'Anyway, that's the story.'

'And everyone else has been cleared?' said Guy.

'Just gossip,' said Fran. 'Shows how dangerous it can be.'

'Will they be allowed to carry on?' asked Peter.

'Yes, after a bit of recasting, obviously,' said Fran. 'The girl who Pinch and Punch would prefer be the Fairy Godmother is actually going to be the Cat, and they've got someone new in for the Godmother…'

Libby and she giggled. A groan went round the rest of the table.

'No, no!' said Fran. 'Not that! A star!'

'Who?' came the chorus.

'Dame Amanda Knight!' shouted Fran and Libby in unison. 'Happy Christmas!'

Proudly published by Accent Press

www.accentpress.co.uk

38029346R00070

Printed in Poland
by Amazon Fulfillment
Poland Sp. z o.o., Wrocław